Mel Bay Presents

Joe Venuti
"Never Before... Never Again"

Violin transcriptions by Aidan Massey
Edited by Richard Niles Romano

Cover photo courtesy of Swing Cat Enterprises.

CD contents

Joe Venuti – Violin, Tony Romano – Guitar

1. You Know You Belong To Somebody Else [3:24]
2. Feeling Free and Easy [3:51]
3. Almost Like Being in Love [2:56]
4. Autumn Leaves [3:43]
5. I Want To Be Happy [3:47]
6. Summertime [2:54]
7. I Remember Joe [2:27]
8. An Interview with Tony Romano

1 2 3 4 5 6 7 8 9 0

Visit us on the Web at www.melbay.com — E-mail us at email@melbay.com

CONTENTS

AIDAN MASSEY

Aidan Massey has been on the staff of Junior Trinity for over twenty years, teaching the violin and viola and directing various ensembles including the Symphony Orchestra. He also teaches in the Trinity College of Music Jazz Studies and is County Coordinator for Strings for 'Surrey County Arts' where he teaches the violin and viola, coaches the strings in the Surrey Youth Orchestra and conducts and directs various ensembles. He works as a Jazz violinist with his band 'Cordes en Bleu' and with his duo partner, guitarist Shane Hill and has performed on BBC radio and TV. He runs a popular series of courses and workshops in Jazz improvisation and 'Hot Fiddle' for string players for the European String Teachers Association and Benslow Music Trust.

JOE VENUTI — NEVER BEFORE… NEVER AGAIN
FOREWORD BY RICHARD NILES ROMANO

Joe Venuti was the godfather of the jazz violin. He achieved fame in the 1920's leading various bands with his childhood friend, guitarist Eddie Lang. Both were visionary pioneers discovering the hitherto unexplored territory of jazz on their respective instruments. Their guitar-violin duets and Blue Four and Blue Five sides of the late 20's are considered classics of 'chamber jazz'.

Venuti was also an irrepressible practical joker and many are the strange but true stories of his antics. During the filming of the Paul Whiteman film *King of Jazz* (1930), he emptied a bag of flour into the bell of the tuba and the band seemed to disappear under a white cloud. When the management refused to turn the heating up on a cold night, Joe emptied a van of firewood on the dance floor and served hot dogs to the customers. He threw a piano out of a studio window betting on what chord it would play when it landed. He gave one-armed trumpeter Wingy Manone a birthday present of one cuff-link. On stage with my father he nailed a drummer's foot to the floor because he was playing the bass drum too loudly.

Apart from his own classic Blue Four and Blue Five records with Lang, Venuti appeared on many records by Red Nichols, Frankie Trumbauer, the Dorsey brothers, Bing Crosby and Jack Teagarden. Depressed by Lang's sudden death in 1933 (from a botched tonsillectomy) his career faded for a period. He traveled widely and led an infamously unsuccessful big band.

During the '40's he was a regular on Crosby's radio show and in the '50s he appeared in clubs and began to record sporadically, but never in the guitar- violin duet format until he met fellow Italian-American Tony Romano in 1937.

Born in Fresno, California in 1915, my father **Tony Romano** has had an incredible career as a guitarist, actor, singer, arranger and composer. Beginning at the tender age of 9, in the late 1920's he became a singing star of the popular AL PIERCE RADIO SHOW for many years. His mind-boggling credits include writing songs for Louis Prima, Vic Damone, Anita O'Day and Johnny Mathis, working as vocal arranger for Cole Porter, playing guitar for Bing Crosby, Tony Bennett and Frank Sinatra, acting in films with Errol Flynn and Katherine Hepburn and playing jazz with Benny Goodman and Stan Getz. Romano is perhaps best known for having traveled 6 million miles during WW2 entertaining literally millions of G.I.s as one of the original 4 members of Bob Hope's USO show (with Francis Langford and Jerry Colonna). He went on to perform with Hope in Alaska, Korea, Vietnam and The Dominican Republic.

As a measure of their close friendship and the respect he had for Romano's playing, Venuti gave Romano Eddie Lang's guitar. This was the very first Gibson L5 built to Lang's design to accommodate the new jazz technique he had developed. This guitar with its expressive bell-like tone is heard on this recording.

During the '60s and '70s Venuti began recording more as a leader with Earl 'Fatha' Hines, George Barnes, Zoot Sims, Barney Kessel, Red Norvo and others. A lifetime of hard living caught up with him and he died of cancer in 1978. He will always be remembered as the innovative pioneer and still greatest exponent of the jazz violin.

Never Before…Never Again was recorded by a happy accident. Joe and my father Tony Romano had been playing together at clubs and parties in L.A. in the late 40's – for fun. Romano recalls,

"One day in 1934 I was stopped on the street by an Italian with a violin case. This was not long after prohibition so I thought he was a Mafioso, and he had a voice to match! He opened the large guitar case of my Gibson Super 400 and played a C chord and an F chord. I was a Venuti fan but had no idea what he looked like. Thinking this was a terrible musician, and probably dangerous, I took my guitar and left for a radio date.

"We met three years later in Hollywood on the set of the film *Garden Of Music*. Our mutual friend Johnny Mercer introduced us at 3pm. I had grown up listening to Joe's records, wearing many out trying to figure out what Eddie Lang was playing! Joe and I played for four hours on the set, then went over to a hangout called The Blue Evening and played 'til 2 in the morning! We continued to play together at clubs, private parties, on my T.V. series *Tony Romano's Musical Nightcap*, or at each other's houses when we would meet for 'spags and hot peppers', Joe's favorite food."

In 1954 Mercer had some free time at Gold Star Studios and asked Romano if he and Joe might like to come in and play a few tunes. Joe said he'd do it if Mercer would order hot pepper sandwiches from his favorite deli. They invited some friends to the studio and spontaneously made magic. Joe played his 'Strad', and Tony played his most treasured gift from Joe: Eddie Lang's original L5 guitar.

Venuti's technique was the result of the most rigorous practice, but he didn't like to rehearse with other musicians. Romano recalls, "Joe hated the word 'rehearsal', saying it was an activity only indulged in by 'empty suits with tin ears'! This album was created with the assistance of 1 microphone, 2 bottles of red wine, 4 hot pepper sandwiches and about 40 of Joe's friends, including his optometrist who brought the mandolin!"

The playing? Romano says, "As any violinist living or dead will tell you, Joe Venuti was the greatest!" On *Autumn Leaves* Romano's distant cello-like voice is hauntingly captured on the guitar microphone. On *I Want To Be Happy* and *I Remember Joe*, Venuti plays harmonized lines on all four strings of the violin at once by unfastening his bow and pulling the hairs across the strings.

Many know Venuti only for his early groundbreaking work with Eddie Lang and he would go on to make many records with many different players. But Venuti had always said that Tony Romano's playing inspired him more than any other musical partner. This recording is unique in that Venuti's stunning technique, assured swing, exquisite intonation and voluptuous tone is here joined by a new free-wheeling musical adventurousness informed not only by his solid classical background but by bop and 20th Century legitimate composers.

Famed Jazz critic Leonard Feather wrote on the record's 1979 reissue, "Simple guitar backing was all the violinist needed to trigger a supreme performance and that is what Romano gives him. This is music of the highest and purest order, to which today's so-called jazz violinists should turn in respect and envy. No musician now living is in a class with Venuti or with Art Tatum or the handful of other instrumental geniuses jazz has produced." (L.A. Calendar, 1979) As Romano's son I might be considered biased, but Guitar Player magazine wrote, "Romano's skilled playing behind the legendary violinist is a textbook for acoustic jazz guitar accompaniment, with spirited comping, chord melody, and occasional single note lines and tremelos." (Feb. 1980)

This record is a rare example of sheer joy in music making. Never before had Joe had the freedom of expression he had on this recording - and never again will the world of music have the opportunity to hear these two great artists in full flight.

This is an important publication documenting the artistry of a master at the height of his powers. I hope it goes some way towards reminding the world of music about Venuti and his contribution. I also hope it encourages further study and listening. I grew up as a kid with this crazy genius playing in my living room when I was supposed to be asleep in bed. This book is my way of sharing the exhilaration and wonder that kid still feels when he hears Joe play.

My thanks to Pat Metheny, Bob James, Tim Kiphius, Martin Taylor and Gavyn Wright for taking the time to share their thoughts on this project. I am very grateful to Aidan Massey for his superb transcriptions and annotations, to Paul Anastasio who studied with Venuti for his invaluable input and to Mel Bay Publications for ensuring that this breathtaking evidence of Venuti's mastery is available to music lovers everywhere.

Richard Niles Romano (London, 2004) www.richardniles.com

YOU KNOW YOU BELONG TO SOMEBODY ELSE

Please don't be discouraged by the difficulty of this first number especially by the dazzling fireworks of Venuti's opening cadenza.

• The group of turns at the outset can easily be learned by first perfecting an E major arpeggio up the E string with just your 2nd finger - i.e. G♯ in first position, B in third, E in sixth and so on. When you can do this, playing the turn (23212) in each position is no trouble!

• The fearsome staccato chromatic scale is one of Venuti's specialities. I was first astonished by his skill at this trick in his 1934 recording of the Gypsy tune 'Dark Eyes' but this is a particularly spectacular example. The left-hand fingering is a glissando down the E string (I prefer to use a 3rd finger) until first position is reached, when a conventional chromatic scale fingering takes over. This is coordinated with some kind of off the string staccato. I think that Venuti uses the old Gypsy trick of throwing the bow onto the string in about the middle and pulling a slow down-bow ('saltati'). If you listen carefully, you can hear the bow run out of bounce, but it is done so brilliantly that your ear assumes a continuous staccato for the whole run. If you are the proud possessor of a very rapid 'solid' or 'flying' up-bow staccato (and if you are, I hate you!) you could use that instead. A good effect can also be made with rapid separate bows ('sautill').

• When making transcriptions, you are continually faced with making compromises between readability and accuracy. This was particularly a problem when writing out the many 'colla voce' or 'out of time' passages in this set. The written page can only go so far. Do listen closely to the recordings of all these pieces for answers to any questions you may have about what I've written!

• From bar 1 I have tried to convey some of Venuti's rhythmic freedom, especially the way he anticipates the bar-lines. This makes the rhythms of what is quite a simple tune look quite tricky on the page. I suggest that you try to play such sections strictly in time at first, perhaps with a metronome, before trying to emulate the masters phrasing. You cannot achieve Venuti's wonderful rhythmic flexibility without a strong internal pulse. Kites cannot fly unless you hold on tight to the string!

• Bars 71- 86 form a wonderful study in 'Swing Bowing'. If your background is basically classical it is worth taking some trouble to learn to swing. Many jazz musicians are suspicious of playing with classically trained string players because of our tendency to play behind the beat and our 'rinky - tinky', corny attempts to swing. Let's not let the side down!

Swung eighth notes (quavers) do have a triplet feel - but not quite! Play this:

Did it swing? Does it sound like jazz? Probably not. This is why swing style jazz is not written in compound time. It doesn't convey the essence of swing and furthermore, makes many of the more complex rhythms difficult to read.

Most jazz fiddlers swing by slurring across the beat. Try this:

SWING THE ♪'S

DOO - BAH   DOO - BAH   DOO - BAH

6

Say 'doo-bah doo-bah' as you play it. The slurs need a subtle articulation: slightly accent the start and 'tail off' the end of each slur. Try it just above the middle of the bow and keep your fingers and wrist flexible. The accents should fall between the beats; jazz is a syncopated music.

After you have tried a few more scales like the one above (jazz musicians practice in every key!) how about swinging a Kreutzer study - you know the one!

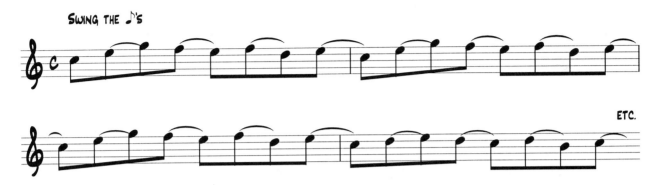

Now try a few characteristic Venuti swing phrases extracted from this set of transcriptions. If you are studying improvisation, find some more, get them by heart and try them in different keys.

Now go back and try bars 71 – 86. Are you swingin' now?

• The cadenza that forms the coda (bars 120 to the end) is Ravelian in its delicacy. (What a wonderful effect when the violin tremolo is below the guitar melody.)

7

You Know You Belong To Somebody Else

Transcribed by Aidan Massey

Joe Venuti and Tony Romano
Hollywood California - 1954

West/ Siras/ Monaco

Cadenza - Freely

♩ = C104 Molto Rubato (Colla Voce)

11

FEELING FREE AND EASY

As you may gather from the title, this delightful Romano/Venuti original is a rather more relaxed affair. There are a few technically challenging moments, but on the whole, Venuti keeps his fearsome technique well in reserve.

• The run in sextuplet ♪'s in the first line is a pattern that is worth memorizing and transposing if you are studying improvisation. Also, the first part of line two is a Gm6 arpeggio. Minor sixth patterns are well worth getting into your playing as you can play them over many chords to great effect. Django's playing was full of them! Check out Mark Levine's essential book 'Jazz Piano' if you want to find out more.

• From bar one, the first 'colla voce' chorus is another wonderful example of 'out of time' playing. Notice how Romano anticipates and compliments Venuti's every gesture.

• In bars 39-42, and later in the coda, bars 91-94 Venuti thickens out his lines by playing in parallel fifths. This is common in jazz fiddle, present too in the playing of Stephane Grappelli, Eddie South and Stuff Smith. It is an easy technique to accomplish if you have sausage-like fingers (like many of the great violinists). If you have slim and elegant hands, don't even try to cover both strings completely; just play on the fingerboard right between them. It is amazing how little left-hand pressure is required to get double stops to sound clearly. (According to Romano, Venuti had rather fat fingers!)

• The double stop passage in bars 63-66 is easier than it looks. The way the notes of the Amajor chord in bar 63 are split 'two and two' allows you to settle the shape of your left-hand in the chord shape securely. Now, keeping you thumb loose under the neck, you can slide the whole shape up in semitones, keeping your fingers down through the whole passage. Don't forget that the ♪'s in the first two bars are swung, even though they are performed with separate bows.

• Bars 95-96 may seem a little 'far out' at first. Like many jazz musicians whose musical language was formed in the 20's and 30's, when Venuti tries something harmonically ambiguous it is usually based on diminished seventh chords, as you will see in some much more ambitious moments in later numbers. Use conventional diminished pattern fingerings to help your intonation here - use 4th fingers on the D♯'s and G♯'s.

Feeling Free and Easy

Romano/Venuti

Joe Venuti and Tony Romano
Hollywood California - 1954

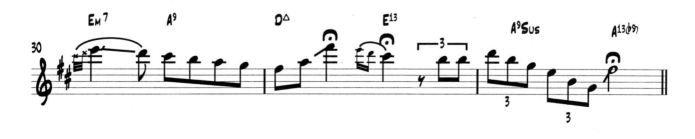

15

16

ALMOST LIKE BEING IN LOVE

This is my favorite performance of the whole set. These two master musicians expose this beautiful Lerner and Lowe theme with the utmost tenderness and respect while adding their own tasteful embellishments right from the start. If it seems too 'corny' for modern jazz sensibilities, you have missed the 'twinkle in their eyes' and the joy of this music making.

• The opening phrase is Venuti's signature tune or call sign as mentioned in the interview with Romano on the disc. It turns up often in his extensive discography. Fourths are such pure intervals they are hard double stops to play in tune. Use first position and as many open strings as possible. You should be getting pretty good at parallel 5th's by now! The runs in bar 2-3 and 108 are thickened out chromatic scales. Use your favorite chromatic scale fingering.

• The syncopated 'pick up notes' at the end of bar16 are signals to the accompanist to change tempo! With effortless skill, a tiny gesture is all that is needed to indicate the new tempo and the change to swing style. It reminds me of the way Louis Armstrong brings in his whole band with two similar pick ups after the opening trumpet cadenza that changed music forever in his 1928 recording of 'West End Blues'.

• The repeated D's in both the violin and guitar parts in the linking passage in bars 26-28 are written in cross-head notes to indicate their indistinct quality. The ensemble is pretty ragged here (nonetheless exciting for that) and it is hard to figure out exactly what is going on. However, I think the rhythms I have written are as close as I can get to the original and sound pretty authentic.

• In bar 62, slide up and hit the G with a 4th finger. When you get to bar 66 stay in 6th position for almost the whole bar, playing the B and G with 3rd and 1st fingers on the A string. Then use the 'ghosted' open A to get down into 3rd position. This is one of numerous examples of Venuti's fluency in high positions. This was no doubt developed, along with his powerful and penetrating tone, so he could be heard when playing with loud 'horns' and drummers, before reliable amplification.

• The straight ♪ passage from the end of bar 81 - 84 is another Venuti speciality known as 'Shuffle Bowing'. The influence of this remarkable instrumentalist is underrated! This technique was copied, from his early recordings and broadcasts, by Western Swing and Texas style fiddle players who play country dance music and the instrumental breaks in country songs. They used shuffle bowing as a brilliant solo feature or as 'comping' (accompanying - making a rhythmical and harmonic backing) behind solos by other players. (I have even heard tell of Celtic fiddlers and guitarists in the Shetlands stealing licks from Venuti and Lang by listening to broadcasts on short-wave radio from 'The Voice of America'!)

The basic pattern of 'shuffle' goes like this:

Play it with very short strokes in the middle of the bow, with a supple wrist and flexible fingers, keeping upper arm movement to minimum. This way, although you will have to go slowly at first, you should be able to speed it up to Venuti tempo! Make the accents firm to emphasize the 'Hemiola' (threes against twos) effect.

Venuti throws in a few extra rhythmic variations of course. Notice also how he outlines the chord changes (the repeated B's become a jazz 11th on F#m).

Just out of interest here is a more typical passage of 'Shuffle' from Venuti and Lang's 1928 recording of their tune 'The Wild Cat'. If you haven't heard any of their work from this era, it's time to check it out; you are in for a tremendous treat! Their original '78' sides are available on CD compilations on several labels - look out for the digitally 'cleaned up' versions. What a treasure house of original musical thinking and instrumental accomplishment!

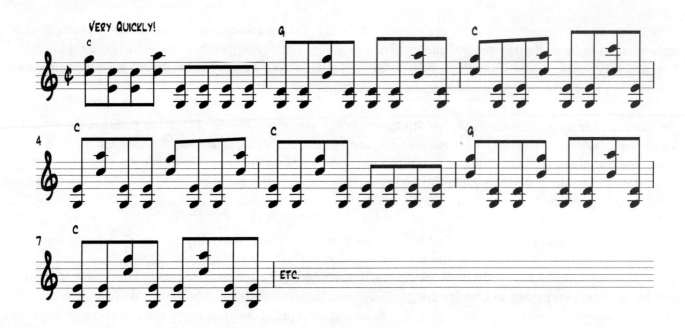

Almost Like Being In Love

Transcribed by Aidan Massey

Lerner/Lowe

Joe Venuti and Tony Romano
Hollywood California - 1954

24

AUTUMN LEAVES

It seems quite fortuitous that this set contains the two songs that are most popular with beginners to jazz improvisation, namely 'Autumn Leaves' and 'Summertime'. They have also inspired great performances from the best players of the idiom. They are both wonderfully easy to play on; new variations and melodies seem to come naturally on their simple and inevitable chord sequences. It is surprising therefore, that Venuti and Romano treat both tunes in quite an uncharacteristically 'non jazzy' way. They make much more reference to the European classical and gypsy traditions, albeit in an ironic if affectionate way.

There is no 'swing style' in this performance of 'Autumn Leaves' at all. Most performances of the tune owe more than a little to the famously swinging recording made by Miles Davis on Cannonball Adderley's 1958 album 'Somethin' Else' and it is interesting to hear a mostly ballad style reading of the tune from four years before it was made. Compare Venuti's 1954 reading to a 1979 performance by the then emerging talent of modern jazz violin Didier Lockwood ('New World' Didier Lockwood - Polygram 821 880-2) and you will see how far this tune, and jazz fiddle traveled in 25 years!

• Venuti leads off in his best expressive style (I stopped marking his first entries with 'dolce expressivo' - everything Joe plays is either 'dolce expressivo' or 'HOT expressivo'!). As soon as the identity of the tune is established he starts to add some heart-rending variations.

• In the second and third choruses, Venuti answers each phrase of Romano's vocalise with some improvised 'parlando rubato' comments.

• The bridge of the tune, from bar 52, becomes an acknowledgement of this tune's gypsy origins.

• The coda is a quotation from Hubay's famous 'Czadas' 'Hejre Kati'. (I am proud to say that Hubay was my teacher's teacher!) How brilliantly and stylishly Venuti plays it!

Autumn Leaves

Transcribed by Aidan Massey

Joe Venuti and Tony Romano
Hollywood California - 1954

Mercer /Kosma/Prevert

In Tempo - Gypsy Style (Straight ♪'s)

ACCEL. -

PRESTO (♩ = C176)

31

34

I Want to Be Happy

You are probably used to this form by now:
1. An introduction in the form of a cadenza for the violin.
2. A colla voce ('out of time') presentation of the main theme of the song exploiting the romantic, improvisatory possibilities of the violin.
3. A tempo change into some red hot choruses of jazz!
4. A coda, usually in the form of another flamboyant cadenza.
'I Want to be Happy' falls into this coherent and satisfying form, with a few minor variations.

• The opening cadenza is very straightforward, in fact beautifully simple.

• The theme that is presented 'out of time' is like the verse of a song, rather than the chorus that everybody knows. By delaying the familiar theme with such a melodious diversion, we experience a delightful feeling of expectation.

• The chorus is introduced in pizzicato chords. Strum these chords hard. Place the bow into your fist, straighten you right index finger and hit all three notes as simultaneously as possible over the fingerboard. A firm left hand will help to make them ring. I haven't insulted your intelligence by fingering these chords; they are all in first position and straightforward. However, learn them well. They appear in a much more challenging context later on!

• There then follows a little over a page of great swing playing. Enjoy!

• The tempo heats up even further at bar 103. Romano's little solo here is to give Venuti time to change to 'Four String Bow Technique' as it takes a few moments to set this up - as explained below. You'll have to practice this change very hard to be ready in six very quick bars! According to Romano, Venuti had been doing it since he was a teenager!

• Joe Venuti's 'Four String Bow Technique'

This is the most famous of Venuti's specialities. I am most grateful to a British violinist called George Hurley for showing me how to do it in a break in a boring orchestral rehearsal. We got to talking when he heard me playing a few jazz phrases while warming up. George played 'hot fiddle' in various London dance bands between the wars. The highly talented multi - instrumentalist, Adrian Rollini (bass sax, vibraphone, clarinet, 'hot fountain pen' and 'goofus'!) worked in London at this time. He was one of Venuti and Lang's close circle, appearing in various versions of Venuti's 'Hot Fours and Fives'. When Rollini brought along some Venuti/ Lang style arrangements, George played the Venuti role.

Hold your violin firmly between your shoulder and jaw. Now, TAKE A DEEP BREATH! Unscrew the bow nut completely until it comes out of the bow stick; remove it and put it somewhere safe so you can find it later. If it hasn't come away already, pull the frog away from the stick. Now the hair should be dangling from the head of the stick like a line from a fishing rod. Hold the bow vertically in your left hand, with the hair facing right. Carefully thread the head and neck of the violin between the stick and hair - keep going until the hair is in playing position, near to the bridge. Grab the frog of the bow with you right hand, and then the stick goes into the same fist, about six inches from the end of the stick. Let go with your left- hand and return it to playing position on the neck. Now you should have the stick underneath your fiddle and the bow hair going over the top! (See photo).

Make sure you don't hold the stick too near the end as this will mean that the stick will rattle on the back of your fiddle and remove priceless varnish! It would be a good idea to practice this with a cheap fiddle and bow to start with - or phone the insurance company!

If you get so good that you want to try this at a gig, I suggest you use two bows - i.e. a cheap bow with the screw removed already for the 'four string' stuff and your best one for all the rest.

Try bowing - you will soon find that 'four string bowing' is rather a misnomer. By changing the angle of your upper arm and hence the angle that the loose band of hair attacks the strings you will find that you can play the strings in various combinations:
1. With a high upper arm you can play just the G and D together.
2. Drop the upper arm a little - you can now play G, D and A.
3. A little lower gets you to the symmetrical position where it is possible to play all four strings at once.
4. Lower still - D, A and E
5. With your arm so low that your elbow is against your body, you can play A and E.

It will take a little practice to isolate the strings you want. Try holding the bowstick further or nearer the end (mind the stick clonking on the back of the fiddle) to change the angles.

Most of Venuti's voicings are three notes only. When fingering a three-note chord it is possible to dampen on the remaining string with the side of a finger any way, so that it doesn't vibrate, so it isn't so important to be so accurate with your string selection.
Now try this three-note chord exercise:

This should help you to coordinate your left hand with this strange new bowing technique. The exercise also explores some of the chord shapes that Venuti most often uses. You need quite a confident double stop technique to make this work - good luck!

Now try one of the less daunting passages from the transcription, say bars 111 - 130, very slowly. (Treat the cross head note as if they were normal, they are just not too clear on the recording.) Do you see how it relates to the earlier pizzicato passage? If you learned this carefully in pizzicato, it should be an easy first ride in four string bowing technique.

• Things really heat up on the next page. Notice how the swung chords are often connected by 'swing bowing' i.e. slurs across the beat.

• Look carefully at the last chord in bar 170. Ignoring the open E's at the top, this chord (from the bottom, C♯ B♭, E) is the first of a row of diminished seventh shapes. If you study these carefully they will become a very good preparation for some sticky moments in the next numbers!

I Want To Be Happy

Transcribed by Aidan Massey

Caesar/ Youmans

Joe Venuti and Tony Romano
Hollywood California - 1954

SUMMERTIME

Venuti and Romano's performance of 'Summertime' has travelled a long way from Gershwin's original. The bluesy lullaby from 'Porgy and Bess' seems to be on a Spanish holiday! (Porgy meets Carmen?)

• After the declamatory introduction, Romano's reharmonization of the theme reinforces the flamenco flavor.

• After the first chorus, instead of improvising on the 'changes' of 'Summertime', they invent an episode based around the Amin tonality of the original, without actually referring to the theme at all.

• In the section bars 33 - 50, the ♪'s are swung rather than the ♪'s. I realize that this is most unusual, but it is due to the way this passage relates to the rhythmic proportions of the rest of the piece. Improvised music doesn't fit neatly into theoretical conventions, - thankfully!

• The 'cross string' arpeggio passage starting in bar 66 is troublesome. The first three bars are fairly easy to figure out, if difficult to play. From bar 71 the tonality is very confused. I think that Venuti is using another diminished seventh shape, sliding it down in semitones. However the distances between his fingers don't stay stable and a few weird intervals result. By bar 74, he seems to feel that it isn't going anywhere, so he abandons ship. He then teaches all improvisers a good lesson: if things sound as if they are getting lost, throw off an impressive run, based on a dominant chord. You will soon find your way home!

• To finish with a cry of 'Ole!' the coda, includes a quotation from Rimsky- Kosakov's 'Capriccio Espagnol'.

Summertime

Transcribed by Aidan Massey

Joe Venuti and Tony Romano
Hollywood California - 1954

Gershwin/Gershwin/Heyward

46

48

49

I Remember Joe

The final number I have transcribed is a tour de force of 'Four String Bowing Technique'. I don't know if Venuti and Romano conceived the rather melancholy little sixteen-bar tune that starts off this number, especially for this set. However, it certainly turns up in later Venuti recording sessions.

• The theme is played once in G, and once again in D - simply one string over. Once you have the basic shape of the tune in your fingers, it is easy to see how he elaborates and varies each repetition.

• After an up-tempo four bar linking passage from Romano that deftly changes key again, the rest of the number is five glorious choruses of twelve-bar blues (starting bar-37) in C. This part of the tune is a catalog of Venuti's four string licks.

• The first two choruses are not too difficult. They use the basic shapes I introduced in my three note chord exercise. Some are shifted about chromatically, but you should find the fingers begin to fall into place quite comfortably, although you will probably need to take a much slower tempo than the recording at first.

• From bar 61 those diminished shapes turn up again. Look carefully at this passage; the way it is constructed is obscured by the rhythm. The diminished chord on the third ♪ should be played on the G, D and A strings. The next diminished chord, on the fifth ♪ is a semitone down from the first. Your hand is then set up to play the next quavers in the same position on the A and E string. The next diminished chord is on the first ♪ of bar 62, again, down another semitone. Then next is on the third, then the sixth and seventh ♪'s , all going down chromatically. Similar diminished chord shapes, with different rhythmic figurations, occur in bars 63 - 64 and 95-97.

• If Venuti's four string technique is new to you and you would like to hear more, I urge you again to check out his astonishing early work on the many CD compilations that are available. Look out for the following tracks: 'Black and Blue Bottom' (1926) 'Sunshine' (1927) 'Four String Joe' (1927) 'Oh Peter' (1931).

By the way, I can recommend a good bow rehairer in England if you get into a tangle!

I Remember Joe

Joe Venuti and Toni Romano
Hollywood California –!954

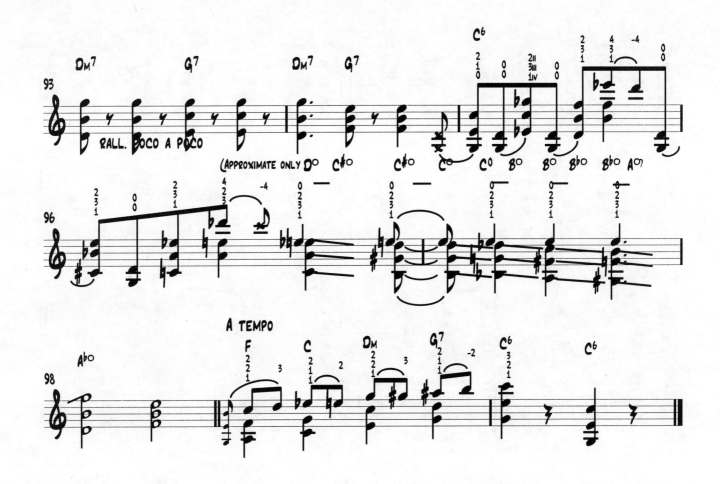